Fia & the Imp

Lauren Mills & Dennis Nolan

Little, Brown and Company

Boston   New York   London

*For Evie May
Love
Mom & Dad*

Copyright © 2002 by Lauren Mills and Dennis Nolan

First Edition

Library of Congress Cataloging-in-Publication Data
Mills, Lauren A.
Fia and the imp / Lauren Mills and Dennis Nolan. — 1st ed.
p. cm.
Summary: Though she is a wingless fairy, Fia does what she can to help her friends, the woodkins,
and proves her worthiness to be Queen when she sets out to rescue two little woodkins.
ISBN 0-316-57412-0
[1. Fairies — Fiction.] I. Nolan, Dennis. II. Title.

PZ7.M63979 Fi 2002
[E] — dc 21   00-054953

10 9 8 7 6 5 4 3 2 1

TWP

Printed in Singapore

The illustrations for this book were done in watercolor with pencil
on D'Arches watercolor paper.
The text was set in Galliard, and the display type is by Julian Waters.

Summer had come to an end, and the woolly-bear caterpillars' wide black bands foretold the coming of a long, hard winter. The woodkins were frantically trying to store enough food to last them until spring, but the chilly autumn winds threatened to drive them into their hollows beneath the beech trees.

Fia, the only fairy without wings, saw that her friends were in trouble, so she used her raft to deliver piles of acorns to the woodkins. Frog devotedly pushed her up and down the river from the Oaks, where the fairies lived, to the south bank of Puffer's Pond, where Woodkin Hollow lay. To speed things up, the woodkins built their own raft, and Fia brought them up to the Oaks to harvest. She coaxed Rat into hauling loads of nuts on his back, and Crow had the job of flying sacks filled with acorns down to Woodkin Hollow.

While the grown-up woodkins pushed carts filled with seeds, the little ones played a game of "Who can kick the acorn back to the hollow the fastest?" However, Lobelia's twins, Mugwort and Juniper, were constantly getting lost in the reeds, which slowed down the whole harvesting operation considerably. Everyone blamed Lobelia, who was near to tears. It didn't help her to see Fia's sister Violet and several other fairies fluttering lazily above them.

The fairies already had rich stores of nuts, berries, seeds, and herbs to last them well into spring. Now they were polishing their wings with the last bit of pollen the asters and Queen Anne's lace could offer. A very upset bumblebee buzzed all about them. The fairies, however, ignored it.

Lobelia squinted up at the fairies and said, "Since ye have wings, and there be so many of ye, it would take no time t'all fer ye to help us woodkins gather what we need fer winter."

Violet looked down and sneered. "*Our* chores are done! 'Tis not *our* fault you don't have wings. Why should *we* pay for *your* problems?"

Lobelia shook her fist at Violet and screeched, "But ye *will* pay! There is always payment fer such . . . fer such . . . IMPISHNESS!"

The fairies laughed and tossed their hair in the breeze.

Fia stepped up on the bank. "Violet," she scolded, "if you are not going to help, you could at least show better manners!"

"Little sister, we *are* showing manners by preparing to look glorious for *your* big engagement party at the palace," responded Violet. "But we are wondering what *you* are doing down in the dirt getting all scruffy and scratchy, when you should be working on making yourself appear *at least* presentable. What will the Prince, *your Kip,* think when he sees his future bride and *Queen* looking like a lowly *woodkin!?*"

"Oh! Kip! I almost forgot," exclaimed Fia. "I'm supposed to meet him at my teahouse! We'll come again tomorrow," she told the wood-kins. Rat rushed over to carry Fia on his back.

On her way, Fia clumsily tried to brush the dust off her feather shawl. *After all,* she thought, *the party isn't until the full moon. Of course I can look presentable by then.*

Kip was waiting at the teahouse with a basket of stuffed mint leaves and honey-filled raspberries. Fia had made the teahouse herself, and Kip had since crafted some chairs from grapevine twigs and moss, which he preferred to the stiff-backed satin chairs he was accustomed to at the palace.

After Fia had poured the tea, Kip unrolled his mother's list of those to be invited to their engagement party.

Fia bit her lip as she examined the list. Finally she said, "This includes all the fairies I know, but none of the woodkins, and they are my friends, too."

Kip nodded. "I thought you might feel that way. Let's add their names."

"But the King and Queen won't want to invite the woodkins to the palace, will they?"

"They must!" said Kip, and so the woodkins' names were added.

To make sure every single woodkin was invited, even the troublesome twins, Fia counted on her fingers, her toes, and two of Kip's fingers. "Yes, that's all of them."

"One more thing," said Kip. "Will you have dinner with me at the palace tonight? I can fetch you here at dusk."

Fia grinned. "I'll be ready," she said, and they quickly kissed good-bye.

Fia was sipping her last bit of tea when Violet dropped down in the chair that Kip had just left.

Fia jumped and spilled some tea on her lap.

"Tsk, tsk," said Violet, shaking her head. "You have so much to learn before you are Queen, Fia. I just don't know how you will manage. The Queen must be dignified, if anyone is to respect and obey her. If I could be of any help . . . "

"None that I can think of," said Fia, putting away her dishes.

Twirling her hair in her fingers, Violet continued. "I just passed Kip on my way here, and he was carrying a scroll. What was he up to?"

"Oh," Fia said blandly, "he just invited me to the palace for dinner tonight."

"But what was the scroll for?" demanded Violet.

"Oh, that? That was just a list of those coming to the engagement party. We added the woodkins' names."

"WHAT?!!" Violet sputtered. She flew up and bumped her head on the teahouse rafter, then came crashing back down into the chair. "Rat whiskers, Fia! That's a mistake, a total disgrace to our family! It is one thing to be their friend but quite another to invite . . . why, it's as lowly as inviting your *animal* friends to the palace!" she said, motioning to Rat snoozing below in the sun.

"Oh! Thank you, Violet, for reminding me," said Fia. "I can't believe I forgot to invite them, not that they will want to come; but an invitation would be most appreciated, I'm sure. I'll just write a quick note to Kip." Fia reached for her parchment and quill.

Violet shook her head with such fury that she could barely speak. "This is the lowest . . . the ver— . . . ooo!" she fumed, and shot up into the trees.

Just then Fia looked down and saw Lobelia, followed by three other woodkins — Woodruff, Birchy, and Verbena — all looking very desperate and out of breath.

"Fia . . . please . . . help!" Lobelia said, gulping for air. "Mugwort and Juniper are gone . . . lost! They were playin' on the raft . . . after I told 'em not to. They were so afraid of gettin' a scoldin' that they steered out into the pond and went downriver past Troll's Crossing." Her voice rose shrilly. "And now thar headin' down the rapids to Haunted Wood!"

"Unless they crash and drown afore they git thar," said Woodruff in his flat, gravelly voice.

"Has anyone gone after them on my raft?" asked Fia.

"Well, no, not yet," Verbena said. "Frog took it back to his pond for you earlier. Daffer's got a search crew goin' on foot."

"Then I will take my raft," said Fia.

"Wait, Fia!" implored Lobelia. "We got to have the *fairies*, beggin' yer pardon, but them that can *fly*, and in a hurry. You know they won't listen to us woodkins. Will ye ask 'em fer us?"

"Violet!" Fia called up into the branches, but Violet flew up even higher. "She can't hear me," Fia said. Then she whistled for Crow, but he, too, was out of earshot. "I'll ask Kip to gather a search party."

After Fia had scribbled a note, she ran over to Rat and patted his sleepy head. "My faithful friend," she said, "we need your help one more time today. Take this to Kip as fast as you can." Rat yawned, Fia popped the note into his mouth, and Rat sped away.

"Now," she said, turning to the four woodkins, "who wants to take the raft with me?"

"Down the rapids?" asked Woodruff. "No one's ever . . ."

"I will go with ye," said Lobelia firmly. The others reluctantly agreed. Fia found Frog, and with some coaxing, he agreed to push them as far as Troll's Crossing.

High up in the oak branches Violet perched, looking down at the
woodkins and holding her nose. She was too high to hear what they
had said, but she saw her sister give Rat the note and then run off with
the others.

"Horrid beasts!" She spat and shook the branch to let an acorn
drop. "I will not allow my sister to embarrass herself OR her family by
inviting the lowest of lowlies. I'll have to stop that animal and snatch
Fia's invitation."

Violet flew after Rat and landed in front of him, but since he was racing at top speed he ran straight into her, and she toppled over.

"Disgusting, filthy beast!" she yelled. She stood up and, with her nostrils flared, promptly plucked rat hairs off her garments. Then she pointed to the note in his mouth. "I will take that for you," she said curtly, but Rat snarled.

"Ratty dear," Violet added in her honey-coated voice, "I can deliver it to Kip sooner than you can." Rat tried to move around her, but in a bee's wink, Violet ripped the note out of his mouth, stuffed it into her pocket, and flew off, tittering.

Rat, not knowing what to do, continued on to the palace and gave the tiny scrap that remained in his mouth to the guards. They looked at it and read only "K." Tossing the scrap to the breeze, they laughed and waved him away. Rat sadly retrieved the scrap and headed back to Fia's teahouse.

Frog pushed the raft across Puffer's Pond while Fia steered with her holly leaf and twig paddle. The woodkins remaining at Woodkin Hollow called out from the shore, "Luck be with ye!"

When Fia and the others reached the river at Troll's Crossing, they all thanked Frog, who stayed awhile on the bank anxiously watching after them. Soon they passed Daffer and his search party slowly making their way along the bank. Then the raft hit the dreaded rapids, and the crew had to use all their might to hang on and dodge danger. The woodkins on the bank stared after them in horror.

Fia's crew fought the rapids all afternoon, and the river grew wilder and wilder. "It can't get any worse!" Birchy shouted, but Fia saw what lay ahead. "Waterfall!" she shouted, and down they plunged. Everyone was thrown off. All the woodkins managed to scramble up on the bank, but they only glimpsed Fia as she was swept downriver and out of sight.

"No!" screamed Lobelia, and all of the woodkins wailed as they saw their friend washed away. "Lost forever," sobbed Woodruff.

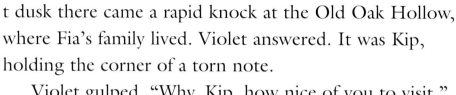

At dusk there came a rapid knock at the Old Oak Hollow, where Fia's family lived. Violet answered. It was Kip, holding the corner of a torn note.

Violet gulped. "Why, Kip, how nice of you to visit."

"Is Fia here?" he asked, looking concerned. Fia's parents and other sisters gathered around.

"But isn't she with you, Kip?" Violet asked nervously. "She told me that you two were having dinner together at the palace."

"True, and we were to meet at her teahouse at dusk, but only Rat was there, with this." He waved the scrap impatiently.

"Oh, that," muttered Violet. "That's just part of this invitation Fia wrote. . . ." She pulled out the other piece and unfolded it. Her voice began to quaver as she read: "Kip — Round up a fairy rescue team — Hurry! Woodkin twins went downriver on raft — Heading toward Haunted Wood! I'm starting ahead on my raft — Love, Fia."

Now Violet was crying. "I didn't know. . . . Oh, that was hours ago, and now it's almost dark and she has no wings — she'll never survive! And it's all my fault! None of this would have happened if I had helped the woodkins. . . . Or if I had answered Fia when she called me. . . . Or if I hadn't stolen her note. . . . Ohhh," she said, sobbing.

Kip turned away and spoke firmly to Fia's parents. "Inform the palace. Have them gather a search party. I'm flying over the river and into that wood."

"Let me come with you!" cried Violet.

"Follow, then," said Kip.

The cold river swept Fia farther and farther, sometimes pulling her under until she was gasping for breath. Finally she crashed into something at the river's edge and dragged herself up onto what she recognized as the woodkins' raft! She searched the mud for any sign of woodkin tracks, and in the fading light she saw two little pairs leading into an awfully dark and uninviting wood.

Haunted Wood. At least they made it this far, Fia thought, shivering so much that she shook her feather shawl dry. She stumbled along in the darkness, feeling for the tracks with her fingers until she reached the knobby roots of an old tree. And there were Mugwort and Juniper, huddled together and shaking from cold and fright. When Fia whispered their names, they squealed with joy.

"Hush!" said Fia. "You'll attract attention, and there are too many dangers here." She scrunched down next to them.

"Fia, can YOU bring us home?" Juniper asked doubtfully.

"No, we'll have to wait for the other fairies," said Fia.

Mugwort cried, "I wish I could be in mama's arms NOW!"

Fia sighed and said, "And I wish I had wings and we could all fly home, but there's no use wishing." She lay down and spread her shawl over them. "Cuddle up now and go to sleep. I'll keep my eyes open for the others."

The twins soon fell asleep and Fia stared up at the sky for a long while, wondering if the fairies had refused to search. *But where is Kip?* she thought as her eyelids grew heavier.

A sudden snicker made Fia sit upright and woke the twins. From behind a root popped a strange woodland creature. He stared at them with gleaming, golden eyes. The twins clutched Fia's arm and whimpered, "It's the imppa . . . imppa . . . IMP!"

"Yes, indeedy-deedy-deedy. I am Boggle the Imp!" he declared.

"What do you want?" Fia asked nervously.

"No, no, no, NO! It's not what *I* want. Boggle is going to give you what *you* want. Boggle is not wicked. Boggle is *nice!* Boggle grants *wishes,* and Boggle knows your *deepest desires!*

"YOU TWO!" he yelled at the twins, causing them to jump straight up. "Do you wish to be safe in your mama's arms?"

The twins both nodded vigorously.

"Then next time OBEY her!" Boggle shouted, and spanked each of them. "Fiddle-dee-DEE-DAH! Back in mama's arms!" Sparks shot out of his fingers, and the twins were gone!

"See, Fia, how *nice* Boggle is?" he asked, moving closer.

"But why did you spank them?" she asked, moving away.

"There has to be payment," he answered simply. "There is *always* payment." Fia looked at him curiously, remembering Lobelia telling Violet the very same thing.

"I know what you wish above all things," Boggle continued.

"All I really want —" Fia began.

"HUSH!" hissed the imp. Then his voice softened. "You would look sooo pretty with wings. You could fly home right now and show them all how very fit you are to be Queen someday. Even Violet would be kinder to you. All your problems solved. . . ."

"How do you know these things?" Fia asked, trembling.

"A grumbly-mumbly bumblebee told me," said Boggle. "Well, Fia, wouldn't you like to have wings? ANSWER ME!"

"Well . . . yes, I would, but . . . "

"DONE! Ha! Ha! Whip-sack-piddly-ox-POP-drop!"

Fia felt herself blasted up into the air over the treetops, and then she began to fall. Without thinking, she flapped her gossamer wings.

"Wings! I have wings!" she cried out joyfully. Fia soared and circled and somersaulted through the twilight sky. She had never felt anything more glorious.

In time, the sky lightened. Had she been flying that long? How could morning have come so soon?

Fia flew over the river looking for Lobelia and the other woodkins, but she could not spot them. *They must be back home and sleeping,* she thought, and flew on until she saw a cluster of fairies gathered below in the Ash Grove. It was Kip, his parents, and her family! She circled above them and, with her heart pounding, made a dive straight down for a grand entrance!

"Ta-da!" exclaimed Fia. She twirled around, merrily showing them her wings, but no one smiled. No one marveled. No one said anything. Then she noticed that Kip was comforting Violet, who was crying. He turned Violet around for Fia to see. Violet had no wings! Then Fia remembered Boggle's words: *There is always payment.*

"No!" shouted Fia. "I NEVER would have wished for wings if I had known Violet would have to go without! NEVER!" she cried, looking around at all their staring faces.

She flew into the air and back toward the Haunted Wood.

"Boggle! Where are you?!" she yelled, racing toward his tree.

"Hee! Hee!" came his familiar laugh, and Fia caught a glimpse of him darting under a root. The passageway closed behind him before she could follow.

"Boggle!" she screamed, slamming her fists into the root. "I don't want these wings! Why should Violet have to pay?!"

"There is always payment!" came Boggle's voice echoing through the trees. "You made your wish. Now you have what you wanted."

"No! No! That is *not* what I wanted! Give them back to Violet!" Fia curled up in a little ball and shook with sobs.

"Fia! Fia! Wake up!" Fia squinted in the morning light and saw Kip. Quickly she turned and saw that she had no wings!

"Oh, Kip! Does Violet have her wings?" she asked.

Kip said, "Of course, she's always had her wings. You must have been dreaming."

Fia shook her head and then saw Violet running toward her.

"Oh, Fia," Violet cried. "I thought you had drowned. How would I ever have forgiven myself?!"

"We searched all night," added Kip, looking pale but happy.

Fairies landed all around them. Some were carrying woodkins.

Mugwort and Juniper woke up, wide-eyed. "Mama!" the twins called. They ran to Lobelia, burying themselves in her arms.

Lobelia could hardly speak through her tears. "Fia, thar 'as never been a more noble fairy or a better friend."

The Queen then cleared her throat, and all eyes went to her. "Any friend of Fia's is a friend of ours," she stated, and Fia and Kip smiled at each other. Then Violet walked over to Lobelia and said, "I will pay for my impishness . . . by helping the woodkins harvest. And I just happen to know where the best acorns are."

Tears ran down Lobelia's cheeks. "I gratefully accept yer offer, not as yer payment, mind ye, but as yer gift."

"We will *all* help the woodkins," declared Kip. "From this day forward, fairies and woodkins will be friends who work together for the good of all."

The king looked at his son proudly. "And *I* say that we shan't wait for the next full moon to celebrate this engagement. Let us celebrate *now* with our new friends. *Everyone* come as you are to the palace for acorn cakes and cherry fritters, and then we shall attend to the woodkins' harvest while the weather's still fair."

Everyone cheered and headed back to Fairy Wood.

Kip swept Fia into the crisp air, and on their return Fia told him all about her strange dream. When she finished, she said, "Lucky thing it was only a dream!"

"But it was a *real* dream!" she heard Boggle's voice whisper in the wind. "A Boggling dream! Hee, hee, hee!" Then gently the voice asked, "Do you *now* have what you wanted, Fia?"

Fia looked all around her at the fairies and woodkins, who were finally friends. And then she looked at Kip, who held her safely in his arms. She smiled and whispered to the wind, "Yes, now I have all I ever wanted."

A happy bumblebee suddenly dipped across their path and flew back to Haunted Wood.